NO PLACE
LIKE HOME

JANET LORIMER

SADDLEBACK
EDUCATIONAL PUBLISHING

QUICKREADS

SERIES 1
Black Widow Beauty
Danger on Ice
Empty Eyes
The Experiment
The Kula'i Street Knights
The Mystery Quilt
No Way to Run
The Ritual
The 75-Cent Son
The Very Bad Dream

SERIES 3
The Bad Luck Play
Breaking Point
Death Grip
Fat Boy
No Exit
No Place Like Home
The Plot
Something Dreadful Down Below
Sounds of Terror
The Woman Who Loved a Ghost

SERIES 2
The Accuser
Ben Cody's Treasure
Blackout
The Eye of the Hurricane
The House on the Hill
Look to the Light
Ring of Fear
The Tiger Lily Code
Tug-of-War
The White Room

SERIES 4
The Barge Ghost
Beasts
Blood and Basketball
Bus 99
The Dark Lady
Dimes to Dollars
Read My Lips
Ruby's Terrible Secret
Student Bodies
Tough Girl

SADDLEBACK
EDUCATIONAL PUBLISHING
www.sdlback.com

ISBN-13: 978-1-61651-203-3
ISBN-10: 1-61651-203-2
eBook: 978-1-60291-925-9

Printed in Guangzhou, China
0310/03-20-10

15 14 13 12 11   1 2 3 4 5

■ ■ ■

Karen closed her eyes.

"When I open them," she thought, "we'll be home! I'll be in my own kitchen with the pretty yellow curtains. The whole room will smell like freshly baked chocolate chip cookies."

Tears trickled down her cheeks. Karen knew her wish wouldn't come true, but she opened her eyes slowly anyway. *Just maybe—* but she wasn't at home. She was still in the cheap hotel.

Karen, her husband George, and their son Andy now lived in one scruffy room. They were lucky to have a bathroom of their own. There were no curtains on the windows. The room had a sour smell. All their food had to be cooked on a hotplate. And worst of all, she had no friends at all here.

But she had to remember the one good thing about this place! Ever since they'd moved here, four-year-old Andy hadn't been sick anymore.

Karen glanced around. She'd done everything she could to make the room look nice. She'd scrubbed the floor and the walls. But she hadn't been able to get rid of the stains and sour smells.

To brighten up the place, she'd tacked up Andy's crayon drawings. The trouble was, most of Andy's pictures were of their old home. And that made things even sadder for Karen.

Karen and George had gotten married five years ago. They'd found a low-rent, two-bedroom apartment in an old building. The young couple had gotten to know their neighbors—people who'd lived in the building for years. Everyone there looked out for each other. The kids played together. The families

4

had become good friends.

George had a good job working in construction, and Karen worked as a waitress. Both of them were satisfied with their home. But after Andy was born, they began to dream about buying a house. They dreamed of having a yard for Andy, a garden for Karen, and a workshop for George.

"Someday," they said, "when we can afford it." They started a savings account for the down payment.

Then Andy got sick. He'd never been a very healthy little boy. From the day they brought him home from the hospital, it seemed that Andy had one health problem after another.

The doctors couldn't figure out why Andy got sick so often. They tested the paint in the apartment for lead. The test came back negative. Karen wanted them to test the carpet to see if Andy was allergic to the fibers. But tests cost money, and their health insurance wouldn't pay for anymore tests.

Karen had to quit work so she could stay home to take care of Andy. With only one income, George and Karen found it very hard to save anything.

They started dipping into their savings account to help pay for Andy's medical bills. Before they realized it, the money they'd worked so hard to put away was almost gone.

Then, to make matters worse, the landlord sold the building. The new owner raised the rent immediately. George and Karen fell behind in their rent payments. There was no way they could afford to stay there. But finding an apartment they *could* afford seemed impossible. They realized how lucky they'd been. Everywhere they looked, the rents were sky high!

The landlord finally evicted them. Karen and George could hardly believe they were homeless! It was a nightmare. They had never imagined themselves living on the streets.

At first, they'd gone to a homeless shelter. Karen hated every minute of it. The noisy shelter was terrible. Too many people were crowded together there. They had no privacy at all. Karen worried all the time that she and Andy would be hurt or robbed while George was at work.

■ ■ ■

Finally, George found this hotel. Here, they could rent a room by the week. Although they now had privacy, Karen still hated the place. It was in a high-crime neighborhood. The neighbors seemed cold and unfriendly. And Karen was homesick!

"In the old place, the tenants were like one big happy family," Karen remembered. "It's true what they say: There really is no place like home."

Then Karen abruptly snapped out of her daydream. She glanced at her watch, and realized how late it was. George would be home soon. She didn't want him to see her tears.

Then the door banged open. Andy ran into the room, pretending to be an airplane.

Karen grinned. It was wonderful to see her son so full of energy.

"Maybe I should start looking for work again," she thought as she set the small table for dinner. "With two incomes, we'd be able to get out of this trap faster. If I was working, we could afford to pay more rent."

Karen felt cheered by that prospect. Then she thought about one of her former neighbors, Theresa. Theresa and Karen had been good friends. Andy and Theresa's son Billy had played together. "Theresa used to babysit. Maybe she could watch Andy while I was at work," she thought to herself.

Karen's depression lifted. She grabbed Andy the Airplane as he flew by and gave him a big hug! "How would you like to go see Auntie Theresa and Billy tomorrow?" Karen asked.

Just then, the door swung open again. George and his friend Buddy tramped into the room. Neither man looked happy. "Bad news," George said.

"What's wrong?" Karen asked, sinking

onto the bed. George dropped into the room's only chair. Buddy plopped down on the floor.

Andy crawled into his father's lap. After giving his son a hug, George looked sadly at Karen.

"It's about our old apartment building, Karen. The new owner is going to tear it down," George said. "He's going to build a fancy high-rise condominium on the very same site. And guess which construction company is going to be doing the work?"

Karen stared at George, trying to take it all in.

George nodded. "You got it! Buddy and I are going to be tearing down our old home!"

■ ■ ■

Karen felt as if she'd been dropped into a deep dark hole. All her hopeful plans for moving back to the old neighborhood suddenly vanished. "But—but what about our friends who live in that old building?" she gasped.

Buddy shook his head. "Everyone's moved

out already. Who could afford the higher rent? The building is empty."

Karen gazed at him in stunned disbelief. "What happened to Theresa?"

"She and Billy have gone to stay with her mom until she finds a new place. You remember Theresa's mom, don't you? She lived around the corner."

Karen nodded. "I—I was going to see Theresa tomorrow." Karen turned to George. "Now that Andy's well, I thought I might try to get my old job back. I was hoping that Theresa might be able to babysit for me."

George smiled at his son. Then he looked at Karen and nodded. "Why not? We could sure use the extra money."

"Theresa could, too," Buddy said. "With her medical bills, she needs all the extra money she can get."

Karen frowned. "That's right. Theresa *did* get sick a lot, didn't she? I wonder if she's strong enough to take care of a rascal like Andy?"

Buddy grinned. "She's doing a lot better

these days. Go see her, Karen. A visit from you would do her good."

■ ■ ■

Later, as Karen washed their dishes in the bathroom sink, she thought about what Buddy had said. Theresa hadn't been the only tenant to get sick. A lot of other people in their old building had come down with one illness or another. "All of us used to joke that we must be allergic to paying rent," she remembered. "But I wonder what the *real* cause was."

The next day Karen and Andy rode the bus across town. Andy talked non-stop about the games he and Billy would play. Karen pretended to listen, but she was looking out the window and thinking about the old neighborhood.

"The whole street is going downhill. Once the building is torn down, I won't want to come back," she thought sadly.

The bus turned the corner and Karen's heart beat faster. There it was! The empty building looked terrible. Weeds choked the dead lawn. Several windows were broken. Someone had spraypainted graffiti on the front door. Karen felt a lump in her throat. When she and George had lived there, the tenants had taken a lot of pride in that old building.

At the next corner, she and Andy climbed off the bus and walked to Theresa's mother's house. Karen was surprised to see Theresa playing a lively game of catch with Billy on the front walk. "Hey, girlfriend, you look *good!*" Karen called out as they got closer.

Theresa shouted with delight. It had been several months since the two women had seen each other.

As soon as the kids were settled down with toys and lemonade, Theresa and Karen caught up on their news. Karen was amazed at how *well* Theresa looked and sounded! "You seem a lot happier," she said. "Are you?"

Theresa sighed. "I miss the old building—but at least I'm healthy now. In fact,

I feel so good, I'm thinking about doing some babysitting again."

Karen burst out laughing. Then she told Theresa about her own plans to go back to work soon.

■ ■ ■

An hour later, Karen walked to the restaurant where she'd once worked.

They needed part-time workers, so she was hired right away. "It's a start," Karen thought to herself.

As she and Billy rode home, Karen began to feel more hopeful. Maybe her plan would work out after all.

Over the next few weeks, things seemed to be looking up. The only dark spot on her sunny horizon was George. He was putting in a *lot* of overtime!

"Why you?" Karen complained one day. "Why are they driving *you* so hard?"

George had just come home from work. Karen saw how pale and tired he looked. Her worry turned to anger when he said he had to go back after dinner to put in a second shift.

George glared at his wife. "Think of the money I'm making," he growled. "I figured you'd be happy about that. It means we can get out of this hole faster and move somewhere—"

He broke off in a fit of coughing.

Karen slammed a glass of water down on the table in front of him. "I told you to go to the doctor," she snapped. "How long have you had that cold?"

"It's not a cold!" George yelled. "How many times—"

Suddenly, they both realized that Andy was watching them. Their son looked tense and fearful.

Karen threw down her dishcloth and ran to her son. "Oh, honey, I'm sorry!" she exclaimed. She knelt down beside Andy. "Daddy and I didn't mean to yell. We just get a little upset now and then."

Andy's brows drew together in a frown. "Don't fight!" he said in the same tone Karen sometimes used on him.

Karen glanced at George, then back at Andy. "We won't, Andy, I promise. Now go play and let us talk."

The trouble was, there was really no place for Andy to play, except in the hall. Again Karen wished that they had a bigger apartment.

George was coughing again. She got to her feet and put her hand on his shoulder. When he caught his breath, she said, "Honey, I worry about you. You've had that cough for a couple of weeks. You need to see the doctor."

He nodded, sipping the water. "I know," he said in a tired voice. "But there's no time to go. We're on a tight deadline to get the old building torn down. Then we have to prepare the site for the new one. It's good money, Karen."

"Not if you're too sick to go to work," she told him. "You've been putting in too much overtime lately. Why can't your boss pick on someone else for a change?"

George shook his head. "It's not just me, Karen. Everyone's being asked to put in extra hours."

Karen groaned. "Okay, but will you *please* go to the doctor?"

"Okay," her husband sighed. "Next week for sure. I'm going to need a couple more sandwiches tonight," he added, shoving his lunchbox toward her.

Karen opened his lunchbox. She dumped out a jumble of banana peelings, dirty plastic wrap, and crumpled up napkins. One thing hadn't changed, Karen thought as she dumped out the mess. George still had a good appetite.

To her surprise, she found something odd buried in the mess. It was a small jar of dirt. Karen held it up, frowning in bewilderment.

"What's that, Mommy?" Andy asked.

Then it hit her. Karen blinked back tears as she tried to smile at her son. "It's just something Daddy brought home," she said in a shaky voice. "It's a jar of dirt from our old home. I think Daddy must miss it as much as we do."

Andy lost interest and went back to

coloring. Karen gazed at the jar a moment longer. Then she shoved it in a drawer, behind some wooden spoons. She knew George wouldn't want to talk about his sentimental feelings.

George reached into his pocket and handed Karen his paycheck. "Would you bank this for me when you have time?"

Karen's eyes widened when she saw the amount. "Is this a mistake? This is more than twice as much as you usually bring home!" she cried.

"I told you that overtime pays off. Which reminds me, Karen—I have to work this weekend, too."

Karen frowned. "But why all the overtime? Your company has a big crew."

"A lot of guys have been out sick," George said angrily. "I told the boss he needs to hire more workers, but he won't listen. It isn't safe for exhausted men to do that kind of work."

Karen sighed as she repacked his lunchbox. To avoid an argument, she didn't say another word about his bad cough—but she was worried about him.

A light knock on the door signaled that Buddy had arrived to pick up George. George gulped down the rest of his dinner, grabbed his lunchbox and gave Karen a quick hug. "Be good," he told Andy as he hurried out the door.

When he'd gone, Karen dropped onto the chair. The little room looked as if a tornado had whirled through it.

She was busy feeding Andy when she heard a loud banging on the door. She sighed. Now what?

Karen went to the door and opened it a small crack. The front desk clerk was standing in the hall. "You got a message from a guy named Buddy," he snapped, shoving a piece of paper through the gap. "He's on his way over. Your husband got hurt. He's in the hospital!"

■ ■ ■

Karen's heart was pounding as she pulled on her coat. "Hurry up, Andy!" she scolded.

"I can't," the little boy wailed, trying to stuff food into his mouth and answer her at the same time.

Karen gazed at her son in despair. She couldn't leave him here, but how could she take him with her?

Suddenly, she heard a light tapping on the door. "When it rains, it pours," she thought. "I can't take much more of this!"

The woman who lived across the hall was standing outside Karen's door. Annie was a single mom with three kids. Sometimes Andy played in the hall with Annie's youngest daughter.

"I heard what the clerk said," Annie said shyly. "I figured you might need someone to watch your boy while you're at the hospital. I'd be glad to."

Karen gazed at Annie in surprise. "I—I don't know what to say," she gasped. "I—I can pay you—"

"That's okay," Annie said with a smile. "I can use the money, but that's not why I'm here. I'd been hoping that we could get to know each other. Maybe babysit for each other now and then."

Karen smiled. "I—I'd really like that. I really haven't made any friends since we got here."

"Me, neither," Annie said softly. "So maybe—" She shrugged, but her eyes looked hopeful. Then she looked away.

"You never said a word to me before," Karen burst out. "I didn't think—"

She broke off, feeling embarrassed. She'd almost said, "I didn't think you liked me." Then she realized that she'd never taken the time to be friendly herself. She hadn't really given Annie any reason to like her.

Annie shrugged again. "I know people here aren't very friendly. We've all got troubles. But if you need me to—I'd really like to help you tonight."

Touched by her neighbor's generosity, Karen opened the door wide. "Thank you so much," she said with a warm smile.

■ ■ ■

Buddy arrived just as Karen was getting Andy settled in with Annie.

"What happened?" Karen asked as he drove his little pickup down the dark streets.

Buddy explained that George had been working on a high scaffold. "All of a sudden, I heard a cracking sound. Then George yelled, and the next thing I knew, he was lying on the ground."

Karen gritted her teeth as Buddy pulled up in front of the hospital. "Hang on, George," she silently prayed as she dashed inside.

"It could have been much worse," the doctor told her. "Your husband is lucky that he's still alive." The doctor listed George's injuries. Then he smiled. "The good news is that he *will* recover!"

Karen tiptoed into the room. George had been sedated and was still asleep. She sat down by his bed, sick with worry as she looked at him. He looked so pale and silent in the soft light.

Buddy entered the room quietly. He stood at the foot of the bed and gazed at George. Karen told him what the doctor had said.

"I told George not to push himself so hard!" Karen said, her fear turning to anger. "That's how accidents happen!"

"Accident!" Buddy made a sound of disgust. "That was no accident!"

Karen gazed at Buddy in shock. "What are you saying?" she whispered.

Buddy glanced around nervously. Then he pulled a chair up closer to Karen and sat down. "George has been shooting off his mouth," Buddy said softly. "When people started getting sick, George complained. He said there was something wrong with the place. He said we needed to bring in experts to figure out why so many guys were getting sick."

Karen frowned. "He didn't mention that to me. What did your boss say?"

"He ordered George to stop stirring up trouble. But George wouldn't let up. He actually threatened to go to the newspapers."

Buddy paused, glancing nervously at the door. "Tonight, after the ambulance left, I took a close look at that scaffold. Someone had messed with it!"

Karen stared at Buddy in horror. Could it be true? Had someone actually tried to *murder* her husband?

■ ■ ■

Karen couldn't stop worrying about what Buddy had said. On the way home, she brought up the subject again. "Think about it, Buddy. A lot of the people who lived in that old building got sick," she said.

"*I* didn't," Buddy pointed out.

"But a lot of the old people did," Karen said. "And a lot of the children. People who are weaker, Buddy." She thought for a moment. "When Andy was sick, the doctors tested our place for lead-based paint," she went on. "There wasn't any—even though the building is really old."

"George told me he was going to get proof that something on the construction site was making people sick," Buddy said. "That was just before he clocked in last night."

"What kind of proof?" Karen asked.

Buddy didn't know. They both fell silent, thinking. Then Karen said, "Maybe we can find out more if we talk to the people who used to live there. Do you know where they all went?"

Buddy thought for a moment. "Most of them, I guess. And I bet Theresa will remember the rest," he added.

"Then we'd better get to work," Karen said. "If anything is wrong with that site, we have to do something about it."

When Karen went to collect her son, Annie invited her in for a cup of tea. "I don't get a lot of company," Annie said with a welcoming smile.

Karen thought about how late it was. Then she decided that the late hour didn't matter. It was high time she got to know her neighbor better.

Over a cup of hot tea, Karen told Annie what had happened to George on the construction site. "Maybe I made a mistake telling Buddy we should look into this," Karen finished. "What's that old saying—let sleeping dogs lie?"

Annie shook her head. "Oh, no, Karen, you can't stop now. Sounds like there's some kind of cover-up going on. That's bad. If a whole lot of people have gotten sick at that place, there *must* be a reason. You need to find out what it is before more people get sick, or—"

Annie broke off. But Karen knew what her new friend was trying to say.

"I just started working again," Karen groaned. "How can I investigate the work site *and* do my job?"

"Maybe I can help," Annie said. "I'm out of work, living on unemployment. So I've got some time on my hands."

Karen felt encouraged. "Maybe Theresa can help, too," she thought.

■ ■ ■

The next day, Theresa and Annie agreed to work together to locate all the former tenants. Buddy said he'd talk to all of the workers who'd gotten sick.

"Karen, you need to find out more about the site itself," Theresa said. "Who knows? Maybe there's something wrong with the soil."

Karen gasped. She remembered the small jar of dirt that George had brought home in his lunchbox. She told the others about it. "I thought it was a sentimental souvenir of our old home!" Karen exclaimed. "But that must be the proof George was talking about."

"We need to get it tested right away," Buddy said. "I'll get it to a lab."

"Can you do some research?" Annie asked. "Maybe find out what that site was used for before your apartment house was built there?"

Karen groaned. "I hated doing research when I was in high school," she said, "but I'll sure give it a try."

Going from the library to City Hall and back again, Karen spent the next couple of days knee-deep in records. When she finally found her answer, she was furious!

■ ■ ■

The Dirt Detectives, as Buddy called them, met at Theresa's house to share what they'd learned. Annie and Theresa had contacted most of the former tenants. They even had a list of who'd been ill and what kinds of illnesses they'd had.

"It's kind of scary when you put it all together," Theresa said. "A lot of people had respiratory problems, like me."

"And like Andy," Karen thought. Then she remembered George's bad cough!

Buddy had talked to most of the workers who'd gotten sick. Some of them had been willing to talk openly about their illnesses. Others were afraid they might lose their jobs.

But Buddy had saved the best—or worst—information for last. It was a report from the lab. "They tested the dirt in George's little jar," Buddy said. "I made the lab guy explain the results to me in plain English. It turns out the soil sample was absolutely *loaded* with poisonous chemicals.

'Hazardous waste,' the lab guy called it."

Theresa drew in her breath sharply. "No wonder we were all sick! But how did hazardous waste get there?"

"I know how," Karen said quietly. Everyone turned to look at her. "I did some digging into the records," she went on. "Years ago, before the city grew, that area was outside the city limits. A manufacturing company in town dumped leftover poisonous chemicals there. Remember that this was a long time ago—before there were laws to protect people."

"Like Love Canal," Annie cried out. "That place in New York where people got *really* sick. It turned out the houses had been built right where a lot of chemicals had been dumped."

Karen nodded. "I've done a lot of reading about this subject. I'll bet you guys didn't know this: One out of every four Americans lives near an abandoned hazardous waste dump."

"You're kidding!" Buddy groaned.

Karen shook her head. "One child in six is at risk for lead poisoning," she went on. "If babies or children chew on something painted with lead-based paint, they can be poisoned. Even older kids can breathe in dust that's become poisoned by lead from old paint."

Karen looked at her friends' faces. She could tell they were thinking about *their* kids!

Karen spilled out one fact after another. Nearly half of America's waterways are polluted. A lot of kids are putting themselves in danger every time they swim or go fishing. And almost half of all Americans live in places where the air is polluted. Many doctors believe that explains why asthma, a serious respiratory disease, is on the rise.

"We have enough information to go to the newspapers," Karen said, "and to the Environmental Protection Agency, too. You can imagine that the guy who owns that site is going to be really mad! But he's going to have to clean it up."

"The construction company will have to do it's part, too!" Buddy exclaimed. "And no matter how good the pay is, working there just isn't worth the risk."

"It could take years and years to clean up that mess," Annie said sadly. "But at least the people who live around that area will be saved from getting sick."

Later, on her way to the hotel, Karen found that she didn't dread going back there quite as much. When she realized why, she smiled at Annie.

"You helped us a lot, my friend," Karen said, "and you also taught me something very important. I always thought of that old building as my home. But of course it wasn't the building—it was the *people!* It's always the people who make a place a home."

* * *

Several months later—thanks to Karen—the cleanup was well underway. George recovered from his injuries, and both he and his friend Buddy had found good jobs on another construction project. And best of all, after a lengthy trial, an outraged jury awarded Karen and George a $5.1 million settlement!

After-Reading Wrap-Up

1. Near the end of the story, Karen had proof that the old building site was contaminated. What did she do with that proof?

2. Why had the old building been such a good place to live?

3. What was the most likely reason George had a bad cough?

4. *No Place Like Home* had two "problems to be solved." What were they?

5. What did Karen learn as a result of her experiences?

6. What do you think will happen to Karen and her family in the next few months? Make three likely predictions.